ASTRO
GRAN

By Nick Ward

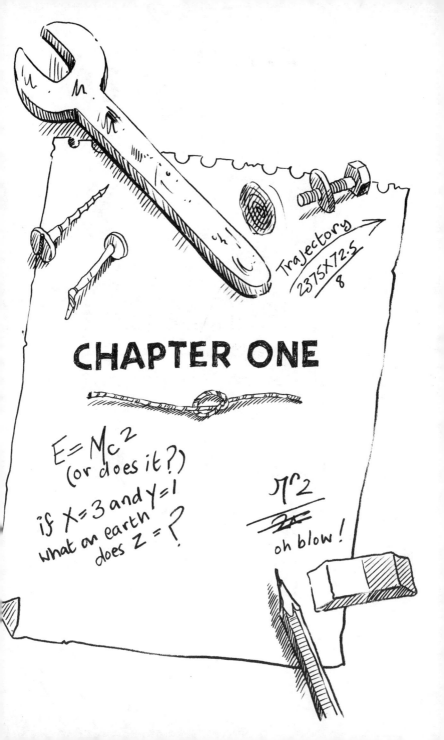

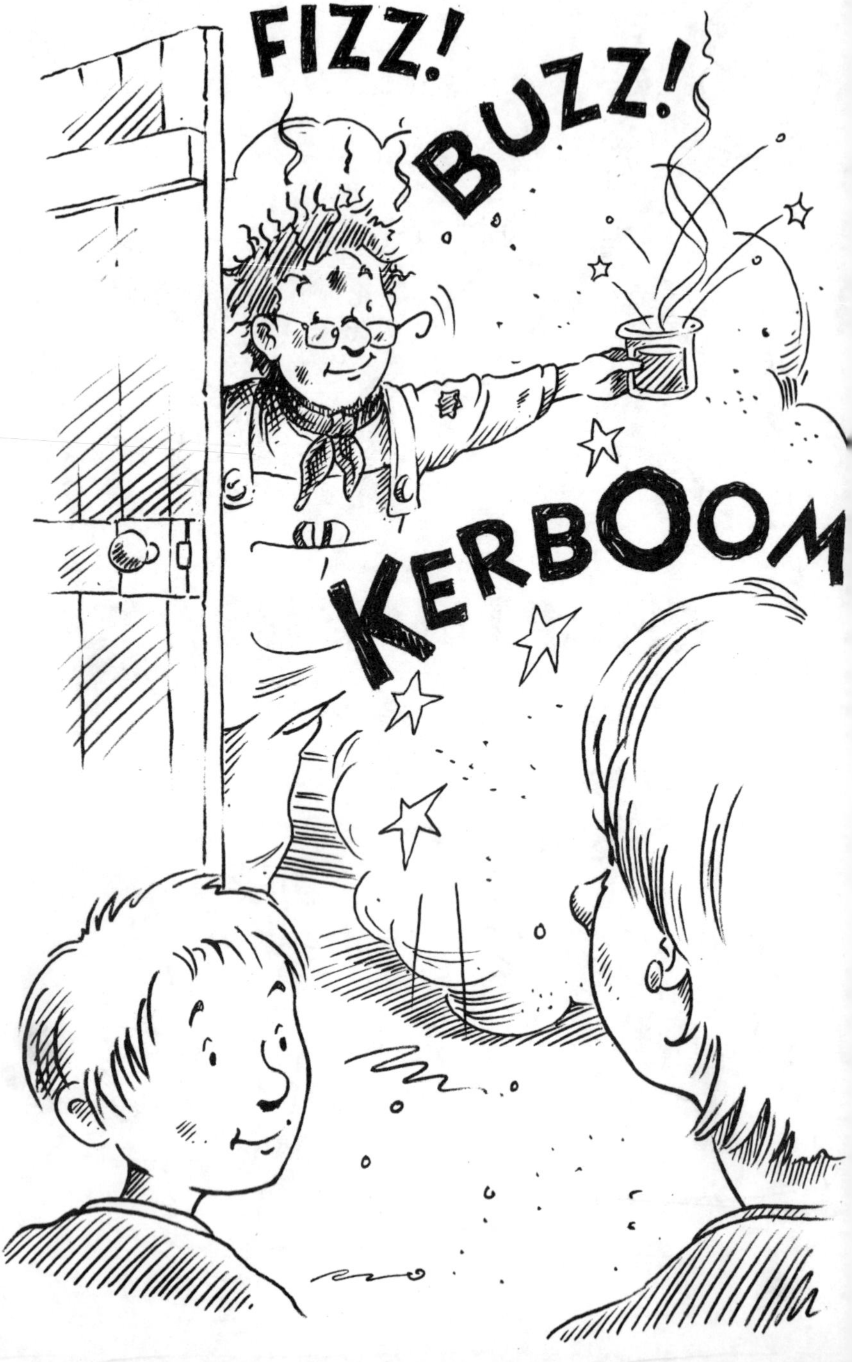
FIZZ!
BUZZ!
KERBOOM

"Oh no," Mum wailed. "Not again!"

"Don't worry," smiled Dad, poking his head around the kitchen door. His glasses were lopsided and his hair was all frizzled and smoking.

"That was meant to happen... really!"

I live with my mum, dad and gran in Horsham. My dad is an inventor, a maker of fantastic gadgets. He spends his days locked in his workshop, designing all sorts of weird and wonderful contraptions. Every week he adds a new invention to the mountain of machinery that fills every corner of our house. Sometimes though, Dad's inventions only half work, and now and then they go horribly wrong! Last week, for example, Dad was busy in his workshop when suddenly...

BABOOM!

A huge explosion rocked our house, sending bits of plaster fluttering from the ceiling and I rushed outside. Dad was sitting on the ground outside his workshop surrounded by clouds of dense black smoke. He looked as if he had just been fired from a cannon!

"Dearie me," he muttered quietly, examining a test tube of brown liquid. "That mixture was a little bit strong!"

"You're not joking," I spluttered.

"Never mind, Rodney. I must try, try again."

"Yes, Dad," I smiled. "What are you inventing this time?" I asked, following Dad into the workshop.

"Oh, I can't say just yet Rodney, but it's something special!" He glanced over at a mysterious shape, hidden under a tatty bedspread.

All morning, Dad mixed and measured liquids in dusty bottles, creating awful smells that made our eyes water and our nostrils sting.

"Phewee!" croaked Dad, choking and coughing after uncorking a very foul-smelling bottle. "This is what I've been looking for. This is the vital ingredient!"

He strapped
on a Second-World-
War gas mask and held
up the large bottle.
Through streaming
eyes I read:

Gran's World-Famous
Pickled Onions
EXTRA STRONG!

"Stand back, Rodney!" shouted Dad from inside the mask. I didn't need to be asked twice and rushed to the far end of the room.

Dad poured a couple of drops into his test tube and, striking a match, held it over the top of the tube.

WOOOOOOSH!

A powerful flame shot into the air, lasted about thirty seconds and slowly died. "Perfect!" cried Dad, tugging off the gas mask and ignoring the huge scorch mark on the ceiling. "Phewee, let's get some fresh air!"

"But what's it all for?" I asked, once we were out in the yard.

"I suppose I can tell you now," sighed Dad contentedly. "I've been inventing a high-powered fuel."

"Fuel? Fuel for what?"

"For Explorer 1," Dad grinned. "My interplanetary space rocket! Come on, I'll show you. The pong should have gone by now."

Dad led me to the mysterious shape in his workshop.

Taking hold of the corner of the bedspread he announced, "Ladies and gentlemen, I give you Explorer 1!" and dramatically whisked away the cover.

Wowee! I couldn't believe my eyes. Explorer 1 was really an old oil-storage tank, almost hidden by a network of exhaust pipes, tubes and dials. A car windscreen had been fitted into the side of the tank, which had been painted a delicate shade of 'Purple Mist', left over from decorating our bathroom. Sitting on top, like a rather wobbly crown, was a satellite dish that had, until recently, been our dustbin lid.

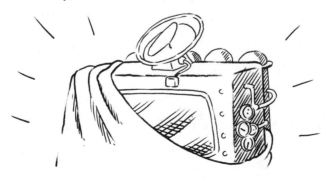

"Well?" asked Dad.

"Er, um…" I was speechless.

"I know," sighed Dad. "It's quite impressive, isn't it? Now all I need is a willing astronaut."

"Dad," I gulped, "you can't be serious. Who would be crazy enough to try to fly this scrapheap?"

Dad was just about to object to my description of his beloved spacecraft, when we heard a noise in the yard.

"We're back, my ducks," Gran shouted. "Who wants a cup of tea?" I saw Dad smile and knew exactly what he was thinking. Gran would have a go at anything.

"No Dad, not Gran!" I pleaded. "You know she can't be trusted to do as she's told. It's too risky."

"Oh, I suppose you're right," grumbled Dad. "I won't mention it."

My gran is quite a character. If she isn't brewing a pot of tea or having a good tidy-up, she's off looking for adventure. Since she came to live with us she's tried skiing, windsurfing, hang-gliding and freefall parachuting.

She isn't very stylish but she always enjoys herself.

That's me, ducks!

"I want some fun," Gran often says. "I'm bored sitting around growing old quietly. I want a bit of zing in my life!"

We went into the kitchen for our tea.

"Ah, lovely. I hope you used my special solar kettle?" Dad asked Gran. This invention was supposed to boil water by the heat of the sun and save electricity. An arrangement of milk-bottle tops and magnifying glasses fixed to an old kettle were meant to catch the sun's rays and heat the water. It didn't work very well.

"No, I did not!" exclaimed Gran. "Load of rubbish! The last time I used that contraption I had to wait two hours for a cup of lukewarm tea. The only thing that boiled was my temper. Why can't you invent something to add a bit of adventure to our lives, instead of boring things to help around the house?"

"Oh, my inventions are boring, are they?" Dad frowned. "We'll soon see about that. Come with me and I'll show you something that will blow your wig off!"

"Oh, Dad!" I groaned.

———

"Finally," said Dad, tapping my boy-scout's compass, "this is the navigation equipment."

We were now inside the rocket, being shown over the controls. They were made from all sorts of bric-a-brac – spoons, taps and ancient telephones. We had already been given a guided tour around the outside and, although Mum looked very apprehensive, Gran's eyes were alight with excitement.

"Very impressive," said Gran, pulling back on the joystick, which was made from the handle of an umbrella. "Will it go?"

"Will it go?" scoffed Dad. "It'll go like, like... well, like a rocket! All I need now is an astronaut. Someone brave and adventurous enough to fly it." He looked enquiringly at Gran.

"That's no problem," she smiled. Again she fiddled with the joystick, making a quiet 'brum, brum' noise, a faraway look in her eyes. "When do I start?"

"Brilliant!" crowed Dad.

"Oh no!" Mum groaned. "It will end in tears, you mark my words."

"Of course it won't," Dad argued. "What could possibly go wrong?"

CHAPTER TWO

What could go wrong? Mum was obviously thinking back to another of Dad's inventions – the Electronic-Eyed-Bird-Seeking-Scarecrow! This robotic terror was designed to patrol the fields of a neighbour's farm, waving its arms frantically and blaring out a tuneless **`BARP´** from a klaxon horn, to scare away the crows. A simple thing, you might think, scaring crows. Not so. The electronic scarecrow blew a circuit and, rampaging across the countryside, ended up scaring the whole street out of its wits.

Nobody spoke to Dad for weeks afterwards.

But Dad was never one to give up. "Try, try again," he always said. He carried on inventing, regardless of any failures or setbacks. And Gran, as I've said, would have a bash at anything. So the next few days were very busy, as Gran prepared for Explorer 1's first flight.

Books were read, graphs were drawn and procedures were learnt. There was a lot of complicated talk about Isobars, Nor' by Nor' West, Dogger and Fishnet.

"Are you sure you understand?" Dad asked Gran.

"I think so, ducky," said Gran, looking very puzzled. "Do you?"

"Of course I do," spluttered Dad. "More or less..."

Soon the big day arrived. With the sun still low in a clear and perfectly blue sky, Dad wheeled Explorer 1 out of the workshop on its pram wheels and into the backyard.

While Dad made last-minute checks to bits of machinery, twiddling knobs and tapping thermometers, Gran was indoors putting on her spacesuit. Finally, checking his watch, Dad called Gran. It was time!

Gran emerged from the kitchen wearing a crash helmet, her pink spotted apron, waders and a rucksack full of supplies. She was ready!

"Now, just remember everything I told you," Dad said. "This is going to be a short test flight, just to get the feel of it, OK?"

"Of course," replied Gran.

Dad uncorked a bottle and poured the contents into the fuel tank. "In you get, Gran. I'll just fill her up."

"Pooh," coughed Gran as the pong of pickled onions wafted across the yard. "That smells very familiar. What is it?"

"Er, secret ingredients, Gran, secret ingredients!"

With Gran safely inside the capsule and the door firmly shut behind her, Dad took me into his workshop. Inside was a bank of ancient wireless sets. They were cracked, dusty and covered in cobwebs. This was Flight Control, where we could keep in touch with Gran during her flight!

"Right, let's see if we can make contact," said Dad, switching on the radio sets.

"Welcome to *Gardening Today*," a voice crackled on the radio. "Today we turn our attention to herbaceous borders..."

"Whoops!" said Dad, and quickly changed the setting. "Hello Gran, can you hear me, over?" After some twiddling of knobs and a lot of squeaks and whistling noises, we got a reply.

"Hello my ducks, Explorer 1 here. Sorry, I was listening to my favourite gardening programme."

Dad tutted. "Are you strapped in, over?"

"Am I strapped in over what?" asked Gran.

"Are you strapped in your chair? Over!" Dad shouted.

"Oh, sorry, yes... over!"

"Right. I am commencing countdown," said Dad. "Please concentrate.

TEN, NINE, EIGHT, SEVEN,

ignition on... um, now where was I?

FOUR... kick the engine starter...

... THREE...

... I said start the engine!"

"I can't," Gran complained. "It's too stiff. You'll have to come and help me, over."

"I can't come and do it," Dad said importantly. "I'm in charge of all this equipment." He turned to me. "Run over and get the engine started, there's a good boy."

Mum was in the yard, hanging out the washing. She had refused to have anything to do with this 'crazy idea', as she called it.

"Where do you think you're going?" she demanded, as I opened the door of Explorer 1.

"I'm just going to start the engine for Gran," I told her.

"Well, be careful," she warned.

"Oh Mum, I'll only be in there for a minute."

I sat in the chair next to Gran and put my foot on the engine starter.

"Ready?" I heard Dad say on the radio. "Right then, ten, nine, eight, seven, six, five, four, kick the engine starter."

I kicked it with all my strength and the engines roared into life. Dad continued his countdown.

"**THREE...** out you come, Rodney."

I pushed at the door – it was stuck!

"**TWO...** Rodney, come out **NOW!**"

"It's jammed, Dad!" I banged at the door and felt the rocket shudder and begin to move.

"**ONE...** turn **OFF** the engines, Rodney!" screamed Dad. "You're rolling down the slope!"

The rocket squeaked down the slope on its pram wheels, hit a flower tub and started to topple. I fell against a lever and knocked it to forward thrust.

Explorer 1 shot through the fence, followed by a huge oily cloud and a revolting stench of pickled onions, and took the washing line and washing with it!

"**LIFT OFF! YIPPEE!**" cried Gran.

I leapt up from my chair as Explorer 1 zoomed across the field next to our house, leaving a scorched and grizzled path through the wheat. We were heading straight for a line of trees at the far end of the field.

"Pull back on the joystick, Gran!" screamed Dad's voice. "**PULL BACK ON THE JOYSTICK!**"

Gran pulled back the joystick and Explorer 1 climbed into the sky, just skimming the top of the tallest tree.

"It works!" we all cheered.

"It really works!"

Soon our house was a tiny dot in the distance.

Mum grabbed the microphone from Dad. "Oh Rodney," she twittered. "Rodney my poppet, are you all right?"

I winced. It was a long time since Mum had called me her poppet!

"Everything's fine, Mum," I told her. "Don't worry."

"But are you sure, stuck up there in that THING?"

"Do stop fussing, you lot," interrupted Gran. "I'm here to look after him, aren't I?"

"That's what I'm worried about," wailed Mum. "It'll all end in tears, you mark my words!"

Up into the skies we zoomed, shredding wispy clouds to ribbons.

"This is the life, ducky," Gran cackled. "Hold on to your hat, Rodney, and let's see what this baby can do!"

She banked the rocket into a tight turn. We climbed higher and higher until Gran released the throttle and sent us diving down again, spinning like a top.

Down, down, down we span and then, just as the ground rushed up to meet us, Gran yanked on the joystick and we soared up in a huge arc and looped the loop.

"Woohoo!" cried Gran. "This beats hang-gliding any old day! Enjoying yourself, Rodney?"

I opened my eyes. I felt very woozy and everything still seemed to be spinning madly. I could only reply with a feeble moan.

"

"Good lad," smiled Gran. "Let's try it again, shall we?"

Luckily, just at that moment, Dad's voice crackled over the radio. "Come in, Explorer 1. Are you sure everything's OK? Now, remember to take it very easy on this first flight. No silliness, PLEASE!"

"Of course not, ducky," replied Gran, giving me a warning look.

Dad and Gran had a long discussion about gaskets and dials and sprockets. We had just reassured Mum that we really were safe, when Dad asked us to state our position.

"We're 35 pounds per square inch, by gas mark 3, my duck," replied Gran reading the instruments.

"That means you are flying directly over Birmingham, over."

Gran looked out of the window.

"Is Birmingham by the sea?"

"No... er, why?"

"There's not a scrap of land in sight!" said Gran.

"Oh, crikey!" Dad panicked. "My calculations seem to be wrong. You'd better come home straight away. Over."

"Typical," we heard Mum say.

"Gran, come home NOW!" barked Dad.

"Not on your nelly," replied Gran. "Over and out!"

She turned the receiver to Radio 1.

"That's better," she sighed, singing along to Madonna. "I've heard enough of him for one day!"

"Gran, shouldn't we do as we're told?" I suggested.

"Oh, not you as well, goody-two-shoes," she complained. "Where's your spirit of adventure, lad? I want to know what happens if I turn THIS!" She pointed to a bathroom tap that was fixed on the control panel. Dad had made Gran promise not to touch it on this first trip. Not for any reason.

"No, Gran!!!!!" I cried. "You promised!"

"I had my fingers crossed," she grinned. Then she turned the tap on full!

"Oooooh!" we yelled as Explorer 1 went into hyper-speed, screamed up into the sky and zoomed off into outer space!

CHAPTER THREE

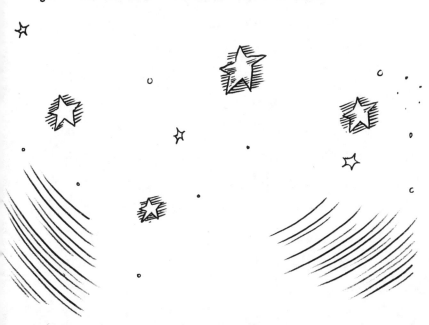

"Gran, are you there? Come in, over."

Back at home, Dad was frantically scanning the dial of his radio set. He just couldn't understand why he had lost contact with them.

"Come in, Gran. Come in, Rodney. ... **PLEASE!**"

"What on earth's wrong?" asked Mum.

"They won't answer me. I seem to have lost them!" Dad replied feebly.

"Oh, brilliant," Mum stormed. "You and your crazy inventions! I knew something would go wrong."

"Nothing can go wrong, Gran's had full training."

"Full training from a prize ninny. You get them back here right now," demanded Mum.

"They can't have gone far, dear, I promise," Dad whined. "They're probably on their way home already."

But neither of them believed it!

We were a long, long way from home, floating like soap bubbles inside Explorer 1 as it cruised through the blackness of space.

"Allez oops," Gran giggled, turning head over heels in mid-air and bouncing off the ceiling. "This is brill! Do you know why we're floating like this, Rodney? It's because there's no gravy up here!"

"Gravity," I corrected her.

"Humph! Same difference, clever clogs," she sniffed.

Then, glancing out of the window, she cried, "Wow, Rodney. Come and take a look at this!"

I floated over to the window and we bobbed there like a couple of balloons, gazing at Earth, brilliant and blue, far behind us.

"Oh, Gran," I gasped. "You've really done it this time."

"Oh, charming. I put a bit of zing into your life and this is all the thanks I get. Moans and groans!"

"But Gran, we must be a zillion miles from home," I cried, starting to panic. "Do you know how to get us back there... in one piece?"

"I should think so, ducky, don't carry on so. Have a bit of faith in your old Gran!"

She chuckled, hovering in the air like a giant bluebottle.

Still, I thought it would be wise to

try to speak to Dad so, with a slow-motion back flip and a sort of doggy paddle, I made my way over to the radio. But it was as silent as space itself.

"It's no use Gran, we're too far away to speak to Dad."

"Good!" she replied. "He'll only spoil our enjoyment. We've got some exploring to do. But first..." she reached into her rucksack and pulled out her trusty old feather duster "... this rocket could do with a bit of a tidy-up."

Gran flitted round the spaceship, flicking her duster over the pipes and dials, humming tunelessly to herself.

"Ah, bliss!" she sighed, floating up to the ceiling. "I wish housework was this much fun at home. I'll have to ask your Dad to invent a flying feather duster."

Gran somersaulted down to land in her seat. "**WHEEE!** Right, let's have a scout round, shall we my duck?" She put the rocket into gear and, with a loud KERBANG from the exhaust, we rattled off into the darkness ahead.

We drifted through space, the only sounds being the gentle crackling of the radio and a rather comforting *Gallupa, Gallupa* from the engine. Everywhere was dark, silent and a little bit eerie.

"Mmm, there's not much up here, is there?" Gran remarked, peering through the windscreen.

"It IS space, Gran," I tutted. "What did you expect, a drive-in McDonalds?"

"No need to be cheeky, young man. I was just thinking we might as well head for home.

"We're not going to have much fun out in space... it's boring!"

"CRACKLE! FIZZLE! POP!"

went the radio. "Help... bzz... Stranded... crackle... No way down!"

Gran and I stared at each other.

"Oh crikey, what's that?" gasped Gran.

Again the radio popped into life. "Calling Headquarters... Engines damaged... Need help!"

"Someone's in trouble, Rodney."

"Oh, well done, Gran," I scoffed.

"Cheek, Rodney, cheek! I wonder who they can be, the poor ducks?"

"Gran, LOOK!" I shouted. "Straight ahead. Wowee!"

There, in the distance, was another spaceship. As we got closer it seemed to grow and grow and grow. It was as big as a skyscraper! Painted along one side were three huge letters: I.S.S.

"What is it, Rodney?" whispered Gran, in a small wobbly voice.

"It must be the International Space Station, Gran," I replied. "I've seen it on the news. They've been in space for months doing scientific tests. They must have broken down."

Gran revved up our engine determinedly. "Let's see if we can help," she said. "Explorer 1 to the rescue! We might get a cup of tea too – I'm absolutely parched."

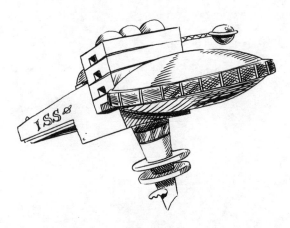

On board the Space Station, the first mate sat at an enormous desk of instruments, desperately flicking switches and pressing buttons. But it was no good. The engines wouldn't start. The Space Station had been bombarded by a storm of meteorites and they were stranded, helpless in space.

Back on earth, Space Headquarters waited desperately for some good news. There was nothing they could do to help the damaged Space Station.

All of a sudden the first mate's heart jumped! What was that? Peering at the radar screen he could see a strange 'blip, blip, blip' getting closer and closer.

"**Captain! Captain!**" he yelled. "**Unidentified object approaching!**"

They rushed to the observation window and, to their amazement, saw the most incredible purple space craft, covered in tubes and pipes, phut-phutting through space.

"What is it, Captain?" gasped the first mate.

"I've no idea, but I don't like the look of it one bit," the Captain replied, lifting his binoculars to get a better look. **"JUMPING JUPITER!"** he screamed, as he saw Gran in her goggles, helmet and spotty apron, waving her pink feather duster at him. "It's an alien! A space monster! Prepare to fire!"

"But we can't fire, Captain. The meteors broke our laser gun too."

"Oh heck, what are we going to do?"

The Captain and the first mate stared in absolute terror at the little purple rocket chugging towards them.

"There's only one thing we *can* do, sir," the first mate gulped.

"What's that?" asked the Captain.

"We must surrender, sir. Invite them aboard and hope they don't blast us out of the skies, just for fun!"

"Surrender? Never!" the Captain screamed.

"They're getting closer, sir. WAVE!"

The Captain watched, goggle-eyed, as Explorer 1 approached. He had no choice. He nervously waved his hand, smiling weakly.

"Oh, look at that," cooed Gran. "They're so pleased to see us, the poor ducks. Wave back, Rodney."

But before I had a chance to stand up and return their welcome, our radio crackled into life again.

"Greetings... um, peace to all. We are friends, please don't fire!"

"What is he blabbering on about?" said Gran. "Sounds as if he's been in space a bit too long!"

"Please make your way to door number seven. You are most welcome to come aboard and join us in some light refreshments."

"Oh, brill," said Gran. "Looks like I'll get my cuppa after all."

She steered Explorer 1 towards a huge door marked '7'. As we got closer the doors slowly opened and we disappeared inside the International Space Station.

Red and yellow lights were flashing on a landing platform, and Gran carefully took our rocket in to land.

"Whoops – a bit of a belly-flop!" she chuckled, turning off the ignition. The engine backfired with a loud belch of exhaust fumes.

"Poooeee!" gasped the Captain. "Whatever they use for fuel, it's disgusting!" He stopped suddenly as the door of Explorer 1 started to open with a rusty creak.

"Now remember, men," he called to his crew in a nervous squeak. "We must be prepared for anything – space pirates, monsters – ANYTHING!"

They gasped as a short dumpy creature waddled onto the platform, followed by a small boy. Gran took off her helmet.

"Hello, my ducks! Have you got the kettle on?"

But the Captain didn't reply. He had fainted clean away!

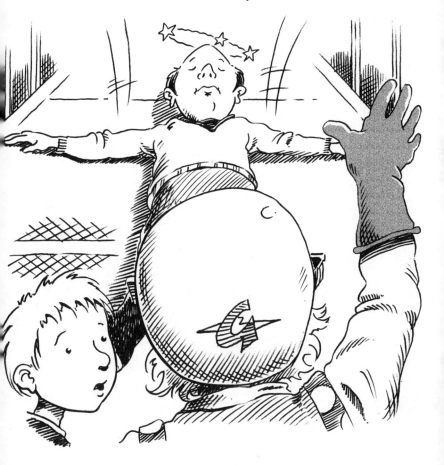

CHAPTER FOUR

"Aaaah!" said Gran, as she finished her third cup of tea. "And that is just about the whole story."

"Incredible!" said the Captain. "Absolutely incredible. You came all this way in a home-made rocket! And you designed it all by yourself you say, Mrs umm, Mrs...?"

"Just call me Gran, ducky, everyone does. Yes, I designed the rocket. It's easy-peasy when you know how!"

"Gran," I whispered. "That's not true."

The Captain didn't hear my whisper and continued excitedly, "That's fantastic, Mrs er... Gran. You see, with your special knowledge and expertise, you might be able to fix our broken engines."

"ME fix YOUR engines? Oh crumbs! Well, I did have a teeny-weeny bit of help from my son, you see, and I haven't got any special equipment here, and..."

"PLEASE, Mrs Gran, you're our last chance!"

Gran looked thoughtful.

"Oh dear," she said nervously. "You are in a jam, aren't you, my duck? I suppose I could have a bit of a think and see what I can come up with."

"Marvellous, Mrs Gran. Thank you so much, I'm sure we can rely on you. I'll go and tell Space Headquarters the good news right away!"

"Gran," I hissed as the Captain led us out of the canteen. "What did you promise to help for? You haven't got a clue about engines."

"He looked so desperate, my duck, what else could I say?" she huffed. "Anyway I might think of something!"

That evening, back on earth, Mum and Dad were trying to watch the telly, but they just couldn't concentrate. Every few minutes they would gaze out of the window at the darkening sky and mutter, "No sign of them yet. They should have been back by now."

Suddenly, something on the TV screen caught Mum's eye.

"Oh no!" she screeched.

Dad turned towards the television.

"Jumping Jehoshaphat!"

His eyes popped and his jaw dropped. There, on the six o'clock news, was a fuzzy picture of two very familiar figures, waving and smiling from the deck of a huge spaceship!

"G... Gran, R... Rodney," he stuttered.

"Ssh," said Mum. "Just listen."

"Space Headquarters has learned that there is hope at last for their

Space Station, which malfunctioned last week," the newsreader said. "Earlier today, the Captain of the International Space Station welcomed aboard two unexpected visitors – a young boy called Rodney and a lady called Gran. Arriving in a do-it-yourself rocket after a long and perilous journey, Gran, the brains behind the rocket, has promised to help save the crew."

"Brains behind the rocket? Bloomin' cheek!" bellowed Dad.

Mum glared at Dad. "You... you silly nincompoop!" she thundered. "'Couldn't have gone far', you said, and there they are stuck up in the middle of nowhere!"

But Dad wasn't listening. "Just fancy," he murmured to himself. "My rocket in space. I never thought it was that good!"

The newsreader continued, "Good evening, Gran. Can you tell our listeners exactly how you plan to help the crew of the Space Station?"

"Well, er... not exactly, my duck," Gran replied from space. "Just give me a bit of time to think and we'll see. As my son often says, I seem to have an answer for everything!"

"We wish you the very best of luck, Gran. Now, I'm sure Rodney must have a message for the nation... Rodney?"

I gulped. I'd never been on telly before. "Um... er, yes," I stammered. "Crumbs, erm..."

"Yes, well, there we have it, viewers," concluded the newsreader. "Can Gran succeed where the experts have failed? I don't think I exaggerate when I say the whole world is depending on Gran to save the day. That's all the news for now. Goodnight."

Over the next few days, Gran and I got used to life on the Space Station, while the Captain and his crew waited nervously for Gran to find a way to rescue them.

The Space Station had a special gravity device so we wouldn't float about. It was so big that we were driven everywhere in funny little space buggies. It was by space buggy that we arrived at the engine room one afternoon, to see if Gran could mend the faulty machinery.

Crikey! The engine room was gigantic, filled with a mass of tanks and motors, sprouting pipes and wires in every direction. Just one look at this maze of mechanical madness and Gran had to admit that she was completely and utterly baffled.

"I'm sorry, my duck," she told the Captain. "I can change a plug and put in a new light bulb, no trouble, but this is a different kettle of fish. It doesn't even look like an engine, it's more like a factory!"

65

"Oh no!" cried the Captain, wringing his hands. "What are we going to do? We'll be stuck up here forever! Never to see a green field again, or a tree, or my mother's dear sweet face…"

"Don't carry on so," tutted Gran.

"It's all right for you," the Captain blubbed. "You can go home in your rocket any old time."

"That's enough of that behaviour, young man," Gran scolded. "We're not going to leave you marooned here in space. Now, where's my feather duster?

A bit of tidying up always helps when I've got some serious thinking to do."

She snatched up her duster and, stepping into a space buggy, cried, "Come on Rodney! Let's not waste time, my duck."

"Do you know how to drive that buggy?" asked the Captain.

Gran gave him a withering look. "If I can drive a rocket, sonny, I can drive anything." She revved the engine and we shot down the corridor.

"Maximum speed twenty miles per hour!" the Captain yelled after us.

"Sorry, can't hear you – I'm a bit deaf!" Gran yelled back, and winked at me!

SCREECH!

We took the first bend at fifty miles per hour, on just two wheels.

"Yippee!" whooped Gran. "This reminds me of the time I raced at Silverstone. Brilliant!" We zoomed down a corridor leading to the canteen. "Gangway!" Gran roared at two waiters, who were wheeling trolleys across the passageway. They dived for cover as we whipped past, leaving the trolleys whirling around and splattering the walls with jelly, mashed potato and brown sauce!

We raced up corridors and down ramps until, coming to a quiet part of the Space Station, Gran slammed on the brakes and brought the buggy to a squealing halt!

"I'll bet it hasn't been cleaned down here for months," Gran tutted, running her finger along a ledge. "You go and amuse yourself,

Rodney, while I do a spot of dusting and thinking."

She opened a door marked 'Special Samples Laboratory. KEEP OUT!' and as I wandered off down the hallway, I could hear her muttering to herself, "It's an absolute disgrace in here. Dust and bits of rock everywhere. It'll be straight down the rubbish chute with this lot!"

Later, I found Gran in the landing bay, staring up at Explorer 1. Our rocket looked tiny and lost in the vast room, its purple paint scratched and flaking. Mum's washing line was still hanging from the top, where it had got caught on our rather wobbly take-off.

"I wonder," Gran muttered.

"Wonder what, Gran?"

"D'you know, my duck," she cried, her eyes blazing with excitement as she unhooked the washing line. "I've got a rescue plan, and it might work. It just might blinkin' well work!"

I frowned. What on earth could she mean?

CHAPTER FIVE

"Tow us home?" shouted the Captain in disbelief.

"Yes, my duck," replied Gran.

"With a washing line?"

"What's wrong with that? It's high-tension line, you know."

"But you can't be serious! It'll never work! It's madness!" The Captain wiped his brow, close to tears.

"Have you got a better idea?" snapped Gran, getting a little huffy. She had expected the Captain to be overjoyed with her wonderful rescue plan.

The Captain was speechless; he just shook his head and burst out crying. He couldn't take any more.

"Come on, blubbering's not going to help," said Gran, patting the Captain's back. "Leave everything to me, my duck. You go and have a nice lie down."

"Yes, thank you, I think I will," the Captain sniffed. "I'm sorry, it's all been a bit of a strain." He shuffled off to his cabin.

"Right," chuckled Gran, rubbing her hands together with glee. "I suppose that leaves me in charge!"

Gran picked up the intercom microphone.

"Attention, attention, this is Gran speaking. I have assumed control of the Space Station. Operation Rescue is about to begin, so please go to your rooms until we have safely landed on Earth."

A loud cheer spread through every section of the I.S.S. as the crew realised that they were going home at last!

Gran turned to the first mate. "Contact Space Headquarters back on Earth, my duck. Tell them we're on our way and will need some rescue ships standing by. I want to land in the sea near Great Yarmouth – it's nice there."

"Yes sir," saluted the first mate.

Taking a space buggy, Gran and I drove to our rocket, which was waiting in landing bay number seven. Tying one end of our washing line to Explorer 1's door knob, and the other end to a railing on the Space Station, we boarded our rocket and started the engine.

"Off we jolly well go!" cheered Gran.

Rising slowly from the platform, Explorer 1 clattered out of the landing bay doors. The washing line snaked out behind us as we flew away from the Space Station.

"Gran," I complained, as I saw our pants, vests and socks flapping about in space. "You could have taken the washing off first!"

"Nonsense," she replied. "It'll give it a thoroughly good airing!"

We shuddered to a halt as the washing line stretched out longer and longer. The Space Station wouldn't budge!

"Oh my giddy aunt," wailed Gran. "It's heavier than I thought."

She increased the revs.

WHEEZE! PUH-PAH! RATTLE!

Our engines strained against the massive weight and clouds of smoke billowed from our exhaust.

"Come on, ol' girl!" Gran shouted. "Come on!"

WHEEZE! PUH-PAH! RATTLE!

Slowly but surely we started to inch forward, gradually increasing speed, and set off across space looking like a little tugboat pulling an ocean-going liner.

"Hooray, good old Explorer 1!" we cheered. "Earth here we come!"

Once we had got the Space Station moving we zipped along quite easily and made the trip back to Earth without too much trouble. We thundered back into the Earth's atmosphere, with the Space Station juddering along behind us like a giant tin can tied to a bicycle. Finally we got through to Dad on our radio.

"Gran?" he cried. "Rodney? Is that you? Oh, what a blessed relief. Well done, you two. Congratulations! You're famous now, you know. Famous all over the world!"

"Oh, it was nothing really," boasted Gran. "Just a little bit of inventive thinking."

"Mmm, that reminds me," said Dad, not sounding quite as thrilled as he was a minute earlier. "What's all this about you being the inventor of Explorer 1?"

"Um, er... can't talk now," Gran stammered. "I'm going to need all my concentration to land this thing!"

The two spacecraft were dropping from the sky like a couple of stones. The grey choppy waters of the English Channel rolled and foamed below us. Suddenly a cluster of parachutes blossomed from the top of the Space Station and it slowed to a gentle glide. The washing line snapped as Gran and I continued to plummet and our laundry whisked away in the wind.

"Rodney...,

THE PARACHUTE!"

yelled Gran.

I searched the controls. Above my head I found a piece of twine dangling from a hole in the ceiling. A luggage label tied to the end said `PULL´. I pulled and *swoosh*, a red-and-white spotted parachute shot out and ballooned above us.

"Just a mo'," said Gran. "Those are my best winter bloomers. What a nerve!"

We plopped into the sea next to the Space Station, which had inflated a giant rubber ring to keep afloat.

"Do we have one of those?" asked Gran, as water started to seep through a small crack under the door.

"Oh crikey, I've no idea, Gran." I grabbed the radio mike. "Dad, how do we stop from sinking?"

"Stop from sinking? Oh lumme, I hadn't thought of that!"

There was a long, silent pause as water trickled across the rocket floor. Gran and I stared at each other, absolutely petrified.

"Just a minute!" cried Dad.

83

"I've remembered. I packed a rubber dinghy, just in case."

"Where the heck is it, then?" Gran yelled.

"Ooh, now where did I put it?"

"Quick, you narna! QUICK!"

"Oh yes, it's at the bottom of a picnic basket, behind the airtanks!"

"Of course it is…" replied Gran sarcastically as I rushed to get the dinghy. "I should have guessed."

We threw open the door and scrambled onto the rubber dinghy, just in time. Behind us, water gushed into Explorer 1. We watched sadly as our trusty little rocket disappeared forever beneath the waves with a loud BLOOP!

"Poor old thing," muttered Gran, a tear rolling down her cheek. Just then we heard the BARP of a rescue ship behind us and, relieved, we climbed on board and began to make our way home to Mum and Dad.

The next few weeks were totally mad.

Dad was right; Gran and I were famous. Everywhere we went, the two of us were treated like heroes. We dined at banquets given in our honour, we opened supermarkets, we appeared on TV chat shows and...

... we even went to Buckingham Palace to meet the Queen. We all had a rip-roaring time!

After a lot of sulking from Dad, Gran finally gave in and admitted that he was the inventor of Explorer 1, and Space Headquarters asked if they could buy his designs. He was as proud as punch and so was Gran because they also ordered one thousand jars of her pickled onions (EXTRA STRONG) to mix with their rocket fuel!

Everything turned out perfectly. All except one thing, that is. Nobody could understand what had happened to the samples of very precious Mars dust and Saturn rocks. They had been kept in a room marked 'Special Samples Laboratory. KEEP OUT!'

"Don't ask me what happened to them," said Gran, crossing her fingers and turning red. "I haven't got a clue!"

It was all very exciting for a while, but Mum, Dad, Gran and I soon started to tire of the bright lights and glamour, the champagne and celebrations.

"I just want to be alone!" said Gran, theatrically.

So we went back to our quiet way of life. Gran returned to her dusting and Mum to her job. I went back to school, worst luck, and Dad started messing about in his workshop again.

A month or two later, however, as we all sat watching a very dull programme on the TV, Gran started to get very fidgety.

"Right, that's it!" she grumbled. "I'm bored, bored, bored! It's weeks since I had a decent adventure. Life's too short to sit around watching rubbish on the telly. It's about time we saw another of your inventions."

"Funny you should mention that," replied Dad smugly. "Come and see what I've been making in the workshop. This will really add a bit of zing to your life, Gran!"

We all followed Dad out into the evening sunshine and over to his workshop.

"Brilliant!" cried Gran when she saw it. "Absolutely BRILLIANT!"

"Oh no," Mum groaned. "Here we go again...!"

Sally Mudgett and the Blue Dragon
written by **Susan Chandler** and illustrated by **Emma Parrish**

Professor Mudgett and his daughter, Sally, live in a little house in a rubbish dump and dream of better things. When one of the professor's 'secret formulas' goes wrong, Sally throws it into the garden and strange things begin to happen. Enter the world of Sally Mudgett and meet the wacky professor, the blue dragon and an evil restaurant owner who likes to be called The Mighty King Poe!

Paperback • £3.99 • 1-84539-100-4

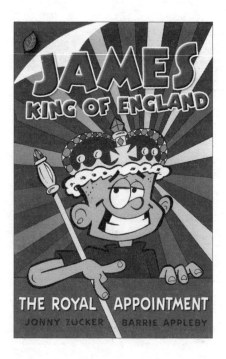

Come in,
come in,
can you hear me?
This book is for Amanda.

Over and out!
N.W.

This edition first published in 2006
by Meadowside Children's Books
185 Fleet Street, London, EC4A 2HS

Text and illustrations © Nick Ward 2006
The right of Nick to be identified as the author
and illustrator of this work has been asserted
by him in accordance with the Copyright,
Designs and Patents Act, 1988

A CIP catalogue record for this book
is available from the British Library
Printed and bound in England by William Clowes Ltd, Beccles, Suffolk

10 9 8 7 6 5 4 3 2 1

ISBN 1-84539-102-0
ISBN 978-1-84539-102-7